# THE
# CARROT SEED
## Story by Ruth Krauss

## Pictures by Crockett Johnson.

**HARPER & ROW, PUBLISHERS**

Copyright 1945, by Harper & Row, Publishers, Incorporated

PRINTED IN THE UNITED STATES OF AMERICA .
ALL RIGHTS RESERVED

Wittmann Library
16801 Yvette Ave.
Cerritos, Ca. 90701

# A little boy planted

a carrot seed.

His mother said, "I'm afraid
it won't come up."

His father said, "I'm afraid
it won't come up."

And his big brother said,

"It won't come up."

Every day the little boy pulled up the weeds around the seed and sprinkled the ground with water.

Wittmann Library
16801 Yvette Ave.
Cerritos, Ca. 90701

# But nothing came up.

**And nothing came up.**

Everyone kept saying it
wouldn't come up.

But he still pulled up the weeds around it every day and sprinkled the ground with water.

Wittmann Library
16801 Yvette Ave.
Cerritos, Ca. 90701

# And then, one day,

# a carrot came up

just as the little boy
had known it would.